To Eva,
Hope you find
squiggles wherever
you go!
~Elizabeth Correll

To Kaia and Quinn, for helping me
view life as a series of sparkles,
squiggles, and simple joys

To Dan, for your endless support and
encouragement

www.mascotbooks.com

The Squiggle Book

For more information, please contact:
Mascot Books
620 Herndon Parkway, Suite 320
Herndon, VA 20170
info@mascotbooks.com

Library of Congress Control Number: 2018914683

CPSIA Code: PRT0819B
ISBN-13: 978-1-64307-281-4

Printed in the United States

The Squiggle Book

Elizabeth Correll

illustrated by Alejandro Chamberlain

Walking along with the breeze in my hair,

I stop for a moment and look up in the air...

only to see a single balloon,

string still attached,

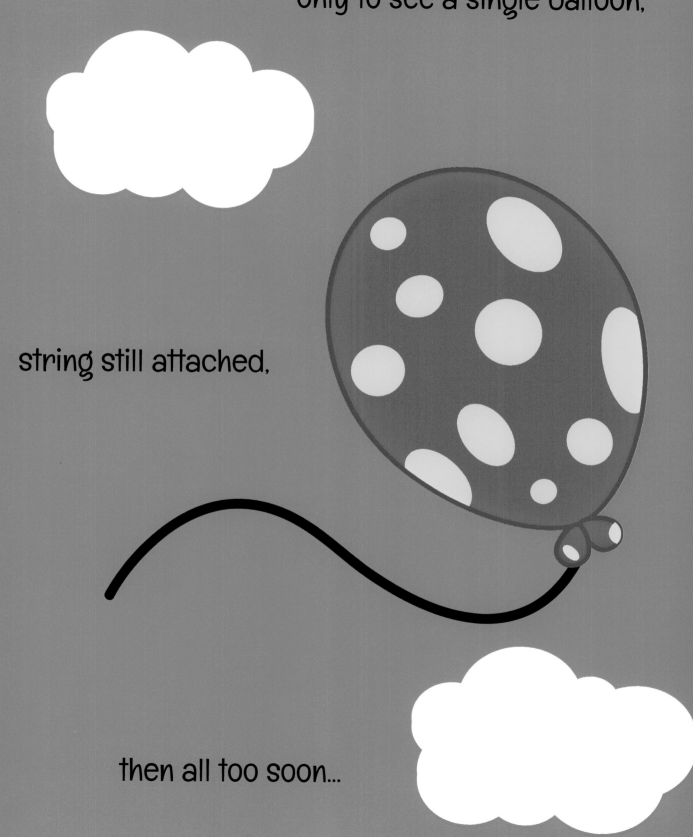

then all too soon...

it disappears into a swirly cloud

as an airplane screams a bit too loud...

and startles a flock of geese flying by—
quite a commotion in the
splendiferous sky!

The sun ablaze, all warm and bright—
its beams break up the big, blue fight...

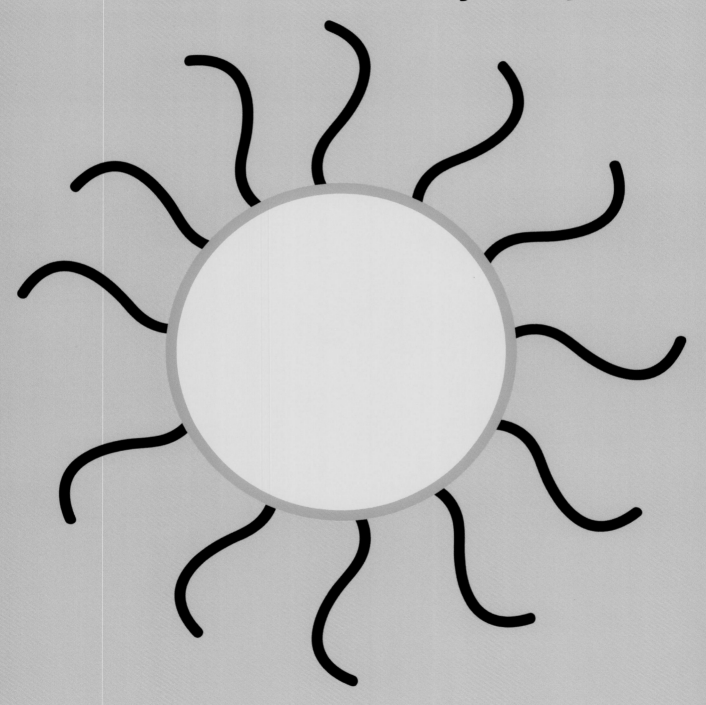

and weave through the trees, making them dance,
loosening up their rigid stance.

A buzz brings me back to the land below,
and I continue to wander,
my mind aglow...

for I can't help but notice this continuous squiggle.
It makes me ponder. It makes me wriggle.

I've seen it throughout my entire walk—
so vivid, so bold...perhaps it could talk?

Do you see what I see?
Quick! Come along with me!
Let's explore the world with squiggle glee!

Look at this squiggle. What do you see?

I see a cheery clown smiling at me!

It could be a snake that slithers on by...

or a colorful kite that flies through the sky!

Let's go for a swim with the fish in the sea...

or ride on a roller coaster—hey, wait for me!

I see a dog. His name is Spot.

Here's a spoon for your soup while it's nice and hot!

Arms of an octopus—two of all eight!

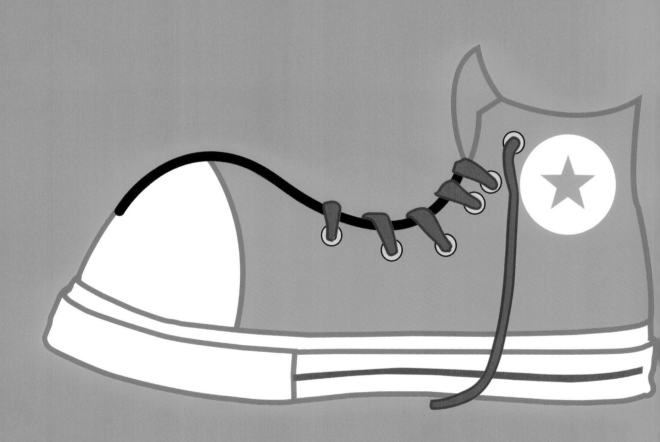

Here is a sneaker, but where is its mate?

A bird in a nest—hear her sing!

Smell the flowers that bloom in spring!

Wave a flag—show your pride!

Pump your legs—swing and glide!

It's a cool new hairdo for a boy named Shane...

The Squiggle Book

or a banner billowing behind a propeller plane!

Flag

Dog

Snake

Flower

Shoe

Spoon

There are so many things that this squiggle can be!
Now it's your turn: Draw what you see!

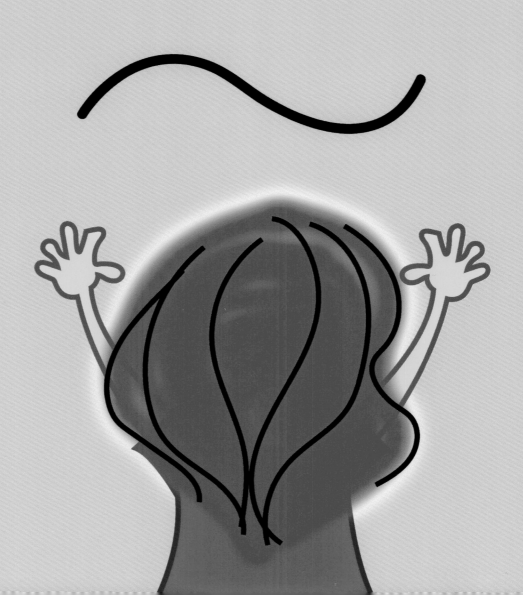

About the Author

Elizabeth Correll lives on Long Island, New York, with her husband and their two kids. She has been teaching fifth grade since 1998 at what she considers her second home, Birchwood Intermediate School. She loves inspiring, motivating, and captivating kids, who energize and ignite her creative spirit and who were the main inspiration for *The Squiggle Book*.

The Squiggle Book is Elizabeth's first book.